Sm51c

COME AWAY
HOME

COME AWAY HOME

◇ ◇ ◇

ALISON SMITH

Illustrations by Deborah Haeffele

CHARLES SCRIBNER'S SONS · NEW YORK
Collier Macmillan Canada · Toronto
Maxwell Macmillan International Publishing Group
New York · Oxford · Singapore · Sydney

Charles Scribner's Sons Books for Young Readers
Macmillan Publishing Company
866 Third Avenue, New York, NY 10022
Collier Macmillan Canada, Inc.
1200 Eglinton Avenue East, Suite 200
Don Mills, Ontario M3C 3N1

First edition   1 2 3 4 5 6 7 8 9 10
Printed in the United States of America

Library of Congress Cataloging-in-Publication Data
Smith, Alison, 1932–
    Come away home / Alison Smith.—1st ed.   p.   cm.
    Summary: Angus, a young sea monster, is blown off course by an
ocean storm and becomes trapped in a Scottish loch, where he is
discovered by Fiona and her dog, James.
    [1. Sea monsters–Fiction.   2. Scotland—Fiction.]   I. Title.
PZ7.S6425Co 1991   [Fic]—dc20   90–41534   CIP   AC
ISBN 0-684-19283-7

To Iain MacLeod
Helen Logan
and Jennifer Smith,
my Scottish connections

◇ 1 ◇

Angus woke up because his tail was hurting terribly. He tried to sit up, but something at the tip of his tail growled and bit down even harder. It hurt too much to bear. He shook his tail with all his might, and whatever had been chewing on it let go and came back down to earth a few seconds later with a thud and a yelp.

He sat up. There was a small black dog shaking sand out of his coat, farther down the shore. The dog gave himself one more shake, braced himself on his short, stumpy legs, and started barking. "You great, ugly, lump, you! Lying on the beach as if you were dead and then flinging yourself about and injuring innocent parties!"

Angus looked around. There was no one else there. The dog meant him. He said, "Were you biting my tail?"

The dog understood him. "What else was I to carry you by?"

Angus snorted. He reached around and gently licked the cut places. Then he started toward the water.

The dog rushed at him. "You must stay till Fiona sees you."

"No."

The dog came closer. His teeth were sharp and white. There were a lot of them. He said, "Fiona must see you." He planted himself between Angus and the water.

"James? James! Where are you?"

Angus turned toward the voice, afraid of what he might see. A human was running toward them from the head of the beach. Angus had been warned about humans since he was the size of a man-o'-war. They were the greatest enemies sea monsters had. He turned back toward the water but the dog stood his ground and bared his teeth. They certainly were sharp and white, those teeth. The dog said, "She's coming. She must see you."

She had seen him. She stopped running, suddenly, and stood halfway down the beach, calling. "James! James, come here to me this minute. Do you hear me, James?"

She started walking toward them, one small step at a time. She had white skin and a lot of red hair hanging down her back. Angus could see that she wasn't any larger than he was, but he felt strongly that even small humans were likely to be dangerous. She was coming closer every second, and there was nothing he could do.

He crouched down, shivering. Fiona stopped in front of him. "Hello." She stretched out a thin arm like a feeler, and touched his neck. "You're crusty!" she said, pulling back. "I thought you'd be slippery."

Crusty? Slippery? This human had some very strange ideas about sea monsters. He glanced with pride at the blue-green scales on his forelegs, and looked again. She was right! He'd been out of the water so long his scales were drying up. Instead of glittering like sapphires and emeralds, they looked like bits of dead seaweed. And the pearly white scales on his chest had turned gray.

Fiona walked around Angus to his tail. "Did you do this?" she demanded of James, pointing with one hand and resting the other on her hip. "Did you?"

James studied the sand in front of his paws.

"You did!" she said. "Well, never mind. I'll get Grandfather's salve that he uses on the cows. You stay here."

James wagged his stub of a tail. Fiona ran up the beach. Angus marveled at the way her feet hardly touched the sand. As soon as she'd disappeared into the trees, he picked up one of his own feet and shoved it toward the water. James bared his teeth.

"She's seen me," Angus wailed.

"She said to stay."

Angus wondered if James could hold on and keep biting while his head was underwater, and, if he could, for how long, but before he could find out Fiona came racing back down the beach. She was carrying a small round thing that glinted in the sun. She scooped a handful of what looked like sea foam out of the round shell and smeared it on the cuts on Angus's tail. "This will make you feel better," she said. "You mustn't be afraid of James. His bark is worse than his bite."

3

Angus wondered how she could say that, with his chewed-up tail right in front of her.

"He used to go hunting with my grandfather," she said, "before my grandfather got too old and had arthritis. Now he's always bringing some wee thing home for me, instead. This time he brought you. There! Does that not feel better?"

It did feel better. The stinging in his tail had stopped.

Fiona straightened up. "I've never seen anything like you before," she said. "Except in books, of course. You're a sea monster, aren't you? Some of the books said you were imaginary, but I always knew that wasn't true."

Angus moved one paw toward the water very slowly. James growled.

"Hush," Fiona said. "Let him away home. If you come back sometime, beastie, I'll have a look at your tail and give you a wee treat . . . if you'll come back."

Angus stumbled into the shallows, then lunged into the deep water. Before the foam from his splash had settled into little floating islands, he was well away from shore. He glanced back over his shoulder. The small human was still watching him, waving good-bye.

Good-bye, Angus thought. Now he could go home. He stopped swimming and looked around. This wasn't the ocean. There was a ring of green hills all around it. If this wasn't the ocean, where was he? His heart started to pound.

◇ 2 ◇

Angus swam slowly in a wide circle, thinking. How had he come to this place? He went around once again and began to remember. There had been a storm . . . a monstrous storm. The wind howled and shrieked. The sea rose into giant waves that hung over him and then crashed down on his head. He'd been tossed this way and that like a scrap of seaweed. The others had submerged and stayed out of harm's way, but he was still so light, he kept bobbing up to the surface.

He'd tried to stay pointed north, in spite of the crashing and tossing about. They had been traveling north in a long line, nose to tail, nose to tail, on their spring migration. They were just off the Scottish coast when the storm hit. . . .

Now he knew where he was. He'd been blown off course and ended up in a Scottish loch. He'd heard about lochs and about the sea monsters who disappeared into them and never came back. Angus shivered. He must find his way back immediately. The others would be regrouping already and looking for him, but they couldn't wait long. Migration was a tide, and a summons, and had to be obeyed.

He swam along the shore of the loch, slowing down now and then to raise his head and cup his ears for sounds of the sea. The sea after a storm was a wild thing and took days, sometimes, to wear itself out and become calm.

The sun was halfway down the western sky when he heard it at last—a hushed, rhythmic roar. The wind was bringing it to him over the mountains. If he could hear the ocean, the ocean and everyone in it ought to be able to hear him. He would call, and someone would come to show him the way home. Each sea monster is born with his own call. Any other sea monster hearing a call is bound to answer, and help.

So he called and listened as he swam. The sun sank lower and lower in the sky. Whenever he looked to the west he felt a little frightened; the day was going by so fast.

Finally, he heard something. A thin, delicate call, so light it almost got lost in the wind. And there it was again! But it was not a call from the sea. It was a bird-call. A small bird, soft brown on top, creamy white below, was clinging to a piece of driftwood wedged between some rocks. Every incoming wave broke just below her and splashed up over her. Angus knew she must be near the end of her strength because she didn't fly away from the waves. He swam over to her very slowly. Birds were easily frightened.

He said, "Would you like me to put you on the shore?"

She closed her eyes, and for a moment Angus thought she was going to fall right into the waves. He took her very gently in his mouth. He could feel the tiny hammer of her heart beating against his tongue. He set her down on some pebbles well above the water.

Her eyes blinked open as Angus stepped back.

She said, "Thank you. I was getting tired . . . getting cold." She tried to fluff out her feathers.

"Was it the storm? Were you blown off course?"

"Yes. Such a terrible storm."

"Will you be all right now?"

"Yes. I think so." She raised her wings as if to fly, but one wing collapsed awkwardly below her and she had to draw the other one back down to her side. It took her another moment or two to pull the injured wing into its normal position.

"Don't move," Angus begged. "I'll carry you higher."

He picked her up again, and hauling himself along, carried her a few feet to a young birch tree. He hoped its cloud of tender green leaves would hide her from enemies and protect her from the wind and sun.

"Is this all right?" he asked. You never could tell about birds. In some ways they were so strong—flying across whole oceans without stopping to rest; and then, sometimes, they were so delicate, dying suddenly like a bubble breaking.

She said, "This is perfect."

Angus stumbled back into the water and began swimming and calling again. The last sliver of the orange sun slipped down behind a black mountain. Darkness began to flow across the loch. He was still trapped. Still lost. How long would they wait for him?

◇ 3 ◇

He swam and called a few minutes longer, but he was tired and his throat hurt . . . it was hard to keep going. Why hadn't someone heard him and come to show him the way out? Maybe the storm had swept him miles away from the others. Maybe they'd already given up and started north without him. He felt cold all over at the thought. On top of everything else, he was getting hungry. Very, very hungry.

Angus sighed. Usually when sea monsters were hungry the whole family would form a circle around a school of fish, and swim in, tightening the circle and trapping the fish inside it. There was always plenty for everyone, and leftovers, even though a great many fish got away. But one sea monster, all by himself, could not form a circle.

He tried chasing a nice fat fish, but it escaped into the deep, dark brown water before Angus could even work up to full speed. Fish were like quicksilver.

A breeze ruffled the surface of the loch and brought

land smells to his nose—the earth, and green things growing . . . and something else. Angus turned into the wind and sniffed again. Something good to eat. Something delicious! He started following that smell.

It beckoned him into the little beach where he'd met James and Fiona. He crawled a few feet up on the sand, weak and shaking with hunger.

James came out from under the trees, poking his nose into this and rooting around that. When he saw Angus, he stopped exploring and trotted away under the trees. A moment later, Angus heard him barking furiously. Angus was backing into the water, preparing to escape, when Fiona came out from under the trees. She was carrying a flat white thing that looked like a giant clamshell, and it was piled high with small brown shells. James was walking beside Fiona, looking up at her. Angus sniffed deeply. That delicious smell was coming from that clamshell. He stopped backing up.

Fiona laid the clamshell on the sand near Angus and stepped away. "I'm glad you came back. I was hoping you would."

Angus moved a little closer to the shell.

Fiona said, "I see that your tail is mending."

Angus was almost at the shell now. That smell was making his mouth water.

James said, "What's holding you? Are you not hungry?"

"I'm terribly hungry. Are these for me?"

"Aye."

"To eat?"

"Aye."

"But they're not moving."

"They're scones," James said. "You'll have a long wait before they move. They're no alive, laddie. They're like biscuits. . . ." He shook his head. "Like oatcakes . . ." He shook his head again. "Fiona makes them every day. She didn't know what sea monsters ate. Why don't I just have one, to give you the idea of it?" James picked up the top scone and backed away with it to a dry spot. He ate it in three bites.

Fiona said, "James! They're not for you."

Angus picked up a scone with his teeth. It was crisp and tender, and warm and salty and sweet, all at the same time. He reached for another, and another, and another. Fiona was watching him, smiling. James said, "Stop when you get to the plate, laddie. The plate's not for eating."

Angus finished the last scone, and sighed contentedly. His stomach had stopped hurting.

"Are they not grand?" James said, licking his little black lips.

"Very grand."

"There's a wee crumb right there by your paw. I'll just clean that up for you."

"Thank you," Angus said, although he would have liked that crumb himself.

Fiona picked up the plate and stroked Angus's neck once, very lightly. "Will you not come back again, beastie? James and I are always here, are we not, James?"

James looked off across the loch. His tail was not wagging.

Fiona patted the top of Angus's head. "I told Grandfather about you, but he wouldn't believe there was a wee sea monster in the loch. He said not to talk like that or people would think I was daft." She sighed.

Angus hauled himself back into the water. Fiona waved good-bye.

He swam to the nearest island. He would spend the night there, instead of floating about on the loch and ending up on the shore again. Someone else might find him sleeping and try to take him home.

He looked back. Fiona and James had disappeared. The beach was just a little glimmer in the darkness.

◆ ◆ ◆

The island was covered with ferns and mosses, which were softer to lie on than pebbles and sand. But the island trees met over his head. It frightened Angus to have something hiding the sky and the stars. Tomorrow night, he promised himself, he'd be floating in the middle of the ocean while the biggest sea monsters kept watch and the stars spun slowly overhead.

He dreamed. At first, he dreamed that he was being rolled over and over, and tossed around, and the air was so full of water and spray and wind that he couldn't tell whether the sea was over him or under him, or even when it was safe to breathe. Then he was caught in a current that pulled him down, down, down, and carried him, still struggling, through water where there was no

13

light. He woke trembling, and howling with fear, and sat up staring all around him.

He remembered where he was. He remembered yesterday and how he got to the island. The morning sun was sending long, transparent fingers through the trees. One of them fell on Angus and warmed him. He stopped trembling.

◆ ◆ ◆

He chased several fish and actually caught one that dashed away from him into the shallows instead of heading for deep water. But one fish, even a large one, was not enough to make his stomach stop hurting.

The wind was blowing across the loch from Fiona's beach. Angus caught a whiff of peat smoke, and scones baking. He headed that way. James was waiting for him. "I thought the scones would bring you in, beastie."

"My name is Angus."

James's bushy eyebrows went up. "Is it? And what will you be doing today, Angus?"

"Going home. I must get back to the sea before they go north without me."

"How will you go back?"

"I don't know. There must be a way. . . ."

"Do you mean the river?"

"I do," Angus said, feeling hopeful. "Where is the river?"

"I wouldn't go down the river, laddie." James looked very serious. "There's men fishing all along the banks. And then there's the falls."

"What do you mean—the falls?"

"The river flows down over a lot of rocks, as if it were coming down a great staircase. Nothing but the salmon can get up and down the falls, even at low water. At a time like this, when the water is high . . ." James shook his head. "Hoosh! You can't see the rocks for the spray it's throwing up."

Angus sagged. He hadn't come into the loch by going up the falls. He'd remember that. "I didn't come in by the river."

"There's no other way."

"Yes, there is." His dream came into Angus's mind. Maybe it hadn't been a dream. Maybe it had been a memory of how he'd gotten into the loch. There must be a river James didn't know about . . . an underground river, flowing under the mountains out to the sea. That's how he was going back.

◇ 4 ◇

While Angus gulped down his breakfast scones, he thought about the underground river. He would look for it where he'd heard the sounds of the sea on the wind. That would be the part of the loch closest to the sea. He finished off the last crumb of scone, said a hasty good-bye to James, and crawled back into the water.

When he reached the right spot, he took a deep breath and dove down the steep wall of the loch. The water grew darker and colder immediately. Still, Angus could see crevices and holes large enough to let him into the face of the cliff, and he could taste salt in the water, so somewhere nearby the sea was coming into the loch. Angus got more and more excited.

He searched for the biggest opening in the cliff, coming back to the surface again and again for air. At last he chose a hole so large he had to stretch his legs out to the sides to touch its edges. He went back up one more time for a deep breath, and then he dove and entered the hole.

Right from the first moment, ledges and pointed rocks scraped his sides and poked him in the darkness. Angus wished he could see where he was going. But in a few minutes, he would be out, and have the whole ocean to swim in.

The water was getting saltier. Angus began to imagine how it would be when he rejoined the family. Everyone would crowd around and exclaim over him and say, "Hush, now, and let Angus talk. . . ." or "Tell us about it one more time, Angus. . . ." instead of asking him to go somewhere else or quiet down. He could hardly wait.

It worried him a little when his legs began to brush the walls of the passageway with every stroke. It was definitely getting smaller. But he would be out soon so that didn't really matter. He peered ahead, hoping to see a little brightness, and swam a little faster.

The passageway turned sharply and grew even smaller. Just for a moment, Angus wondered if he might have chosen the wrong one.

He was running short of air. How long was this passageway? How small could it get?

All of a sudden, it got very small indeed. So small Angus had to stop. He'd made a terrible mistake. He'd have to go back.

He tried to turn, but there was more of him from nose to tail than there was from side to side, and the passageway was too narrow. Angus was so frightened he could hardly think.

He'd have to back out. It would be very hard, with

four stumpy legs and a long tail stuck on behind, but it was the only way.

Backing around the sharp curve, he could feel dozens of his scales being rubbed off. He was going to have to breathe soon. This was too slow! He'd have to turn around now or he'd drown.

He wiggled and pushed, and squeezed and pulled in, and finally, with one last desperate effort, he turned. He swam as fast as ever he had in his life, smashing into rocks, bouncing off walls, never slowing down for an instant. Now he could see a faint brightness ahead. The water was getting fresher. If he could just get out of this awful tunnel before he had to breathe . . .

He was out! There was daylight above him. He went streaking up through the water and came to the surface gasping and coughing. He'd made it.

For a long time he rested on the surface, taking in deep, deep breaths of the green-scented air. Then he turned and looked up at the mountain that stood between him and the sea.

◇ 5 ◇

Angus swam to Fiona's beach late that afternoon. James was sitting on the sand. The scones were already baking. Angus could smell them.

James got up and came to meet him. "Whoosh!" he said. "You look as if you'd been buried, and dug up a lot later."

Angus nodded, embarrassed. "I got stuck, James. I almost drowned trying to get out. That's how I lost my scales." He shivered, remembering. "I thought I'd found an underground river to the sea but I picked the wrong one. Were you waiting for someone?"

"Waiting for someone? No, no. I was just . . . sitting."

"Oh." Angus curled up in a casual coil beside James. He wasn't aware of falling asleep till Fiona, putting down his evening scones, woke him.

◆ ◆ ◆

While Angus ate, Fiona sat beside him with a large book in her lap. Every so often, she would look down at the book, then up at Angus. He didn't mind. He ate a dozen scones and drank a bowl of something called cream which was delicious. Just as he finished it, James told him that Sarah, Fiona's cat, usually got the cream.

"Will she mind, do you think, my having it tonight?"

"Aye. She'll mind."

"I didn't know it was hers. Will you tell her that?"

"Aye. But it won't do any good. She'll be out of sorts, anyhow."

Fiona leaned toward Angus. "This is a book about sea monsters. It's got lots of pictures in it, and one of them looks just like you." She settled back with her book. "I wish you could understand what I'm saying. I showed it to Grandfather, but he got angry with me for talking about you again. He's afraid they'll think he's not rais- ing me properly." She sighed. "I'm not to mention you ever again. That's a shame, isn't it? I think it is."

Angus licked her hand.

James growled. Angus drew back. James was jealous.

She turned the page. "It says that sea monsters get to be fifty or sixty feet long. You must grow awfully fast. And here's another beautiful picture—in color. But you don't breathe fire. Do you?"

Angus tried to see the picture Fiona was looking at, in case it was of a sea monster he knew, but he couldn't see it without getting close to Fiona and he knew James wouldn't like that.

She turned another page and frowned. "It says here you can sing." She looked at Angus. "Is that true?" She smiled. "I wish you could sing for me."

Angus wanted to sing for her, of course, but what kind of song would be appropriate? Fiona wouldn't want to sit through one hundred and two verses of "When Sea Monsters Ruled the Seas." And Angus thought that whale songs were better when actually sung by whales. But that song about seabirds, where he got to imitate them, and the ship's foghorn, and a bell buoy—that would be nice. He took a deep breath and launched himself into "The Song of the Seabirds."

He could tell Fiona was impressed. When he got to the part where he imitated the storm petrels, and the snow geese, and the arctic terns, her eyes got big, and he knew that she recognized their calls. When he got to the sad part where the petrel died, and its spirit went straight up through the clouds to fly forever in the blue above, James began to howl along with him. Fiona leaned forward and stared at them with her mouth open.

When he'd finished, and James had managed to stop howling, Fiona said, "I think you understood me. I really do. I can hardly believe it. Oh, how I wish Grandfather could have been here! And you certainly can sing." She stood up and brushed off her skirt. "I've got to get more books."

◇ 6 ◇

Next morning, James appeared under the trees just as Angus came out of the water. He trotted over to Angus and sat down, panting slightly. James spent his mornings exploring.

Angus said, "I've decided I'm going down the river today, James."

"What? Are you daft?"

"I don't think so," Angus said slowly, trying to remember what *daft* meant.

"Did I not tell you about the men fishing?"

"You did. I'll wait till it's almost dark, then."

"And did I not tell you about the falls?"

"I think," Angus said, "that if salmon can go up and down those falls, so can I."

"Many of them cannot. They try, but they cannot."

Angus could see that James's bushy little eyebrows had knotted together and were sticking out like wee black shelves. He said, "We're very strong swimmers,

James. We can swim where the waves are so tall they come between us and the sky. I'll be all right at the falls. Don't worry."

"Worry? Worry! It's nothing to me if you go down the falls."

Sarah the cat, the color of the brightest coral in the warmest sea, picked her way carefully over the damp sand and sat down beside them.

"He's away down the river this night," James said, darkly.

"Will he be having my cream again, before he goes?" she asked.

"Hoosh! Is that all you can think about?"

"How will he see, to go down the river at night?" she asked.

"Oh, I see well enough at night," Angus said.

"Not as well as a cat can," she said.

"Better," Angus insisted. "Much better."

Sarah stood up and stalked away. The tip of her tail twitched with irritation.

Angus sighed. He was always upsetting Sarah.

James said, "Don't bother with her. Now listen to me, Angus. Go down the river if you must, laddie, but go slowly. Swim a wee bit, and stop, and then swim a bit more. Don't let the river take you."

"I'll go slow," Angus promised. "How will I know which is the right one? There are rivers all around the loch."

James shook his head. "Only one flows away. It'll be over there across the loch, near those three big trees.

There's a marsh around the trees, and an opening in the marsh. You'll feel the water flowing past you toward the trees. Go with the water. Once you're through the marsh, you'll be on the river."

"I wouldn't want to make another mistake," Angus said.

James started to say something and stopped. He sighed. "Ah, well . . . you'll remember to go slow, will you?"

"I said I would." James was frightening him, and Angus didn't like it.

◆　◆　◆

Angus was sleeping on his island, resting up for the trip downriver, when a delicate little whistle woke him. The brown-and-white bird was standing beside his ear. Angus scrambled to his feet. "Hello. How did you get here?"

"Oh, I can still float, and I can run along the shore. I manage very well."

"I'm going out to the sea tonight, down the river."

"No. Don't try the river."

"There isn't any other way. Have you ever seen another way out for a creature like me, bird?"

She said, "No," sadly.

"Well, they'll be going north without me." Angus shook his head. "I'm leaving as the sun sets."

She said, "The river is full of danger. Don't go down the river." Then she darted away through the ferns and disappeared. A few moments later, her

24

sweet, sad call came back to him from the loch. "Please."

He fell into a restless sleep. When he woke, he decided that he had dreamed the bird's visit. He was always dreaming these days—sad or frightening dreams. This had been just another dream.

◇ 7 ◇

He spent the rest of the afternoon imagining his triumphant return to his family. Once in a while, when he thought about the river, a little needle of fear stung him, but he tried to ignore that.

It seemed to Angus that the sun lingered too long in the western sky and refused to set. Finally when the afterglow was tinting the clouds overhead pink and crimson and lavender, he started swimming toward the spot James had pointed out to him.

When he was almost there, he looked back across the loch. He saw a small, black lump on the beach. Could that be James? Above the trees, a delicate column of gray smoke lifted into the sky. Fiona was baking scones. Even though no one might see him, Angus raised a paw and waved good-bye.

As he approached the three big trees, he saw the marsh James had told him about, and when he got very close, he saw a narrow break in the reeds . . . a channel the river had kept open for itself. Now he felt the current beckoning him very gently to go with it . . . to swim into the marsh away from the loch. He let it take him. When he glanced back over his shoulder, a minute later, he could not even see the loch beyond the tall water grasses. He was on his way!

The marsh gave way to a steep hillside that was split by a rocky gorge. The river had to narrow and deepen, and flow much more rapidly through the gorge. But Angus found it exciting to be carried along like this, plunging from one deep pool to another, sliding over slippery, water-polished rocks, bumping into mysterious shapes in the dusky light.

Now he was going very fast indeed, bobbling down a glen roofed over with trees. It was quite dark between the steep, rocky banks. Angus found it easier to let the river carry him where it would than to try to control his own passage. He was getting bumped around a good deal, of course, but the faster he went, the sooner he'd be back in the sea.

His nose picked up the familiar, salty scent of the sea. He must be almost there. He heard a low roar ahead of him. At first he thought he was hearing the surf already, and his heart bounced in his chest with happiness and excitement. Then he realized that this was a different kind of roar. It was the falls he was hearing. And they were getting closer rapidly. Angus decided to slow down. After all, he'd promised James that he would go slowly.

He tried to grab a pointed rock as he whizzed by, but the rock was covered with wet slime and it slipped from his grasp. He tried backpedaling, but the river carried him right along anyway as if he were a bit of foam. He knew now that he was absolutely powerless in its grasp. The sound of the falls was getting very loud. Angus peered ahead, looking for anything he might grab as he flew by. Through the half-light of the gorge he saw a thin, pale gray line stretched low across the river—a branch, maybe, or an old dead tree. He was coming down on it very fast. He struggled to get his forelegs and head and neck well up and out of the water, to be ready to reach for it.

He stretched up and toward the limb as it came at him. It caught Angus hard in the throat, but he was so grateful to have it holding up a part of him, he barely felt the pain. He hooked his chin snugly over it—an old dead tree that trembled under his weight—and then he heaved one foreleg and then the other onto it. Slowly, carefully, so as not to put too much strain on his sole support and only hope, he inched along the tree to the shore. The river pulled and sucked at his tail as if it were angry at losing him. Once, as he hauled himself across a whirlpool at the base of a rock, he almost slipped back into the water. He clung to his tree till he felt safer, and then he kept on going.

At last Angus made it to the bank. It was a treacherous place—slippery and dank, covered with moss and very steep. Rocks and old tree roots stuck up just high enough to trip him. He shuffled cautiously to the edge of the falls, looked down, and gasped. The river plunged to one rock ledge after another till it fell into a pool far below. And oh, the thunder it sent rolling up the gorge, the clouds of mist it threw into the air, the trembling it caused in the very earth under his paws. Angus knew the sea was just beyond the thunder and the mist, but he could not go down those falls.

He waited for his legs to stop quivering and then he started back the way he had come—clambering over the rocks where the river was narrow and swift, swimming upstream whenever he came to a little side pool of quieter water. It took him a long time. The sun was rising when he reached the loch.

He glanced over at Fiona's beach, still in the dawn shadow of the mountain, and saw that same small black lump on the sand. And it still looked like James to Angus. So he swam over to see, because he wanted very much to talk to someone.

It was James. He'd fallen asleep on the sand with his chin resting on his paws. When Angus whispered in his ear, James woke with a start.

"Hoi!" he said, and stood up quickly. "Is that you, beastie?"

"It is. I didn't go down the falls, James. I was too afraid."

"They'd frighten anyone. You were right to come away home again."

Angus said, "But this isn't my home." He huddled on the sand beside James. "The river was my last chance."

James scratched behind one ear. Then he scratched behind the other. Then he said, "I'll just go up to the house and see can I let Fiona know to bring you a wee bite of breakfast."

Angus didn't answer.

"Hoosh, now," James said, just as if he had, and set off up the beach.

◆ ◆ ◆

Angus slept all day. When he woke, he could hardly move, he ached so. He got up very slowly and let himself down into the loch one piece at a time. He decided to swim over to Fiona's beach and see if she'd been making scones. If he could get his stomach to stop hurting, that would be a start.

Fiona came through the trees just as the sun set. She was carrying a plate full of scones. Angus was so very glad to see her.

After dinner, James said, "What will you do now?"

"I don't know."

The wind was carrying the smell of the sea. All evening Angus had tried to ignore it. Now he gave that up and turned to face the mountain that stood between him and the sea. "I could climb out," he said.

James said, "No! You could not."

"I climbed a little today, coming back up the river." Angus looked down at his paws. They were rubbed raw all over. He wrapped his tail around them to hide them.

James shook his head violently. "You haven't gone from the water to the trees, yet. Can you not see what that mountainside is like—the steepness of the braes and the moor?" James shook his head again. "And the rocks? Do you not see the crags, and the boulders, and the rockslides?"

"I could learn how to climb, James. I could practice every day and go farther every day."

"Can you learn in a summer? Because after the birds fly south there'll be snow and ice on those mountains and even the goats themselves will be having trouble."

Angus hadn't thought of that. Snow. And ice. "Maybe by next spring . . ."

"How big would you be, by then?"

"Oh, very big. As big as MacDuff. As big as the sea monster in the picture in Fiona's book. Fifty or sixty feet, she said."

James said, "Laddie, think what you're saying. Something the size of this MacDuff clambering over those mountains? Why, it's out of the question." James huffed and puffed in exasperation. "If you didn't fall to your death, you'd get wedged in somewhere, or be seen by one of those busybodies with cameras, or"—he shivered—"guns. You'd stand out like a monument up there. No. If you're to climb out, you must do it before the snow falls."

"Before the snow falls, then. And I'll be waiting for the others as they come by, going south." Already Angus could imagine it. How surprised they'd all be to see him. How happy he'd be to see them.

"That's the way of it, then?" James said.

"That's the way of it. I'll start practicing tomorrow." Angus slipped into the loch and headed back to his island. He'd need a good night's sleep if he was to learn to climb mountains tomorrow.

◇ 8 ◇

Fiona brought breakfast early. "I'm away to the city, today," she said. "Grandfather's so stiff he can't do the shopping this week. So I'll be riding in with John the Postie, and I'll come back on the bus and walk the rest of the way. That's not the best part. The best part is after the shopping, I'm going by the library and see have they got any books on sea monsters." She paused for breath. "The library in the city is three times the size of the one in Ben Loohie."

Angus ate twelve scones while Fiona talked and waited for his plate, but when he was through his stomach was still rumbling. He decided he'd better learn to fish before he started climbing mountains. He didn't think you could do something like climbing when you were very hungry.

Back in the loch, he followed a large fish for a while, watching it closely. The silly thing got nervous, always seeing Angus behind it, and swam into a little cove where it beached itself.

While he sat on the sand, cleaning the fish scales off his chin with his tongue, Angus thought about that. Twice now he had gotten a fish so frightened it swam into shallow water where it was easy to catch. If there was only one of him, he could not surround a school of fish, but if he could frighten a lot of fish all at the same time and drive them into a little cove, the cove would do his surrounding for him. He could have a fish breakfast every morning. What could he do to drive fish into a cove? He wasn't big enough to loom up suddenly like an underwater mountain or a whale. Making faces wouldn't work. Anything with a face like a fish wouldn't know an ugly or scary face when it saw one. But noise! He'd always been good at that. He could make lots of noises. He could roar and whistle and shriek and howl. It was worth trying.

He slipped back into the water and swam toward the center of the loch, keeping his eyes open for a school of fish. Looking up, he discovered a small school swimming toward him, near the surface. He waited till they were directly overhead, and then he floated quietly up and turned in their direction. Now he was right behind them. He opened his mouth and turned himself loose.

With his first roar, the whole school shot forward as if it had been jerked on a string. Angus had to swim hard to keep up with them while he whistled and rumbled and howled. Now the bottom was rising below him. Suddenly, up ahead, fish were breaking through the surface and flipping out of the water. Angus's stomach scraped sand, and he was out of the water, too.

The beach was a beautiful sight. It was sprinkled all over with flopping, somersaulting fish. Angus tossed most of them back into the water immediately. Then he settled down to have lunch with the rest.

When he was through, his sides bulged. He was absolutely full for the first time since he'd left the ocean. Even more satisfying was the knowledge that he could take care of himself, now. He knew how to fish.

As soon as he didn't bulge anymore, he headed across the loch to the place where he'd heard the sea most clearly. As he swam, he became aware that he was no longer alone. Several small animals were swimming behind and to one side of him. Every time he slowed down, they stopped and backed away. Angus was careful not to look directly at them or go too fast. It was nice to have company swimming, again.

When he reached the shore he heard a low, excited chatter breaking out behind him.

"I told you he was too big."

"Hush! He'll hear you."

"He will not. Look at his tiny ears."

"Look at your own, you booby—and you hear everything."

There was a short silence.

"What is he doing now?"

"How do I know? You're seeing as much as I am. He's probably just resting."

"I think he's a giant water snake, or an eel."

"With legs? And a hump? Don't be daft. And will you, for the last time, stop your shoving?"

"I was here first."

"Well then, you go and speak to him. You ask him if he's a water snake."

Another silence.

Angus began to turn around, very, very slowly. He wanted to get a wee peek at these two before they left.

"Kipper—he's moved."

"Of course he's moved. Were you expecting him to stand there all day like a rock?"

"He's watching us."

"He's not. He's just sunning himself. His eyes are closed."

"Snakes sun themselves. And his eyes aren't closed. There are little tiny slits at the bottom."

"There are not."

"I can see them well enough." Angus heard a small body bumping across the sand toward him. "You see—there's the one, and there's the other. He's looking at you."

Angus opened his eyes. He was in the company of two young otters. The one who had been standing just beyond the tip of Angus's nose immediately fell over backward. Then he scrambled to his feet and bounced back into the water, chattering and squeaking all the way. "He nearly got me, Kipper. Did you see that? Oh, I knew it was a snake. I told you. He tried to get me. Did you see him?"

The other otter, standing at the water's edge, said, "He's Tommy. I'm Kipper. He worries about water snakes. One frightened him when he was little."

"I'm not a water snake. I'm a sea monster."

Kipper said, "That's worse, then."

Tommy came up for air behind Kipper. "You never believe me. You never ever believe me. But I was right this time, was I not?"

"No. He's not a snake. He's a sea monster."

Tommy uttered a small squeak and dove back into the water.

Angus said, "I'm sorry he's frightened but I never tried to get him."

"Oh, I know that. He thinks a water snake is after him every few days. He'll get over it. Are you passing through?"

"Yes. I'm on my way back to the ocean. I'm going to climb out over the mountain."

Kipper looked at Angus for a moment. Then he said, "Are you daft?"

Tommy bobbed up again, a few feet from shore. Kipper said, "He's not staying. He says he's climbing out over the mountain to the sea."

Tommy's eyes got large. "He's not! He couldn't!"

Kipper said to Angus, "He's right, this once. You'll never be able to do it. You may as well try to fly over it."

Tommy asked, earnestly, "Does he fly, as well?"

Kipper cuffed him. "Of course he doesn't fly. Do you see wings on him?"

Tommy backed away, muttering darkly to himself. Behind Kipper's back, he made faces at his brother.

Angus said, "I know it will take practicing. I'm starting today."

"No, no. It's not possible. Stay in the loch, monster. It's no such a bad place to live. You'll get used to it."

Angus said, "Thank you, but I don't want to get used to it. And I will be able to climb some day. You'll see me going up and over that mountain before the snow falls."

But when he went back into the water, he swam to a bit of shore farther down the side of the loch where there were no otters to watch him or tell him he would never make it over the mountain.

◆ ◆ ◆

He was disappointed, when he tried walking up the new beach, to find that the higher shore was covered with bigger, sharp-edged rocks. They caused him to pitch from side to side as he walked across them. He felt as if he were always just saving himself from tipping over. It was very hard work.

The beach rose to a grassy slope. When Angus was only two-thirds of the way to the grass he had to sit down and rest. His feet were getting terribly sore. These stones weren't very good for sitting, either.

There was a rapid clicking sound off to his left, and he turned to see James coming toward him, jumping easily from stone to stone. "James," he called, "will you come and climb with me?"

James stopped. "Do you climb sitting down?"

"I'm taking a wee rest."

James gave a short, derisive yip, and covered the rest of the distance to Angus. Then he looked pointedly down at the water's edge and back up to where Angus sat, and shook his head.

Angus got up. "I'm ready now," he said, and set off again toward the green, green grass.

◆ ◆ ◆

James had reached the grassy slope, stretched out on his side, and taken a short nap before Angus arrived. Angus lay down beside him.

"Another rest?" James asked, severely.

Angus didn't answer. He just lay there, breathing hard.

James said, "You'll no get far if you keep lying down."

"You took a rest."

"Aye. But I had to wait for you."

"Well, now it's my turn." As soon as Angus could stop panting, he got to his feet—his tired, aching, rubbed-raw feet—and started downhill.

"You're not going on?" James asked.

"No."

James pointed himself toward home and left.

Angus hobbled across the rocks with his eyes on the cool waters of the loch. Oh, if he could just float over that mountain—how lovely that would be.

◆ ◆ ◆

As he was swimming back to his island, Angus heard singing like the chiming of a small bell behind him. "You did very well." It was the bird. He knew that even before he looked over his shoulder.

"No, I didn't. I only got to the grassy part."

"I saw you. It's hard."

"Oh, yes. It is. James doesn't know how hard it is."

"Yes, he does," she said gently. "He knows that very few would even try it."

Angus stopped swimming for a minute. "Do you think I'll ever get back home, bird? I have only till winter comes."

"No one can say but you."

Angus started swimming again. He'd hoped for a little encouragement.

As if she'd read his mind, the bird said, "I told you that you'd done very well today."

Angus didn't answer. Why was he so angry with her?

She said, "I couldn't lie to you."

When he looked back, she was gone.

◇ 9 ◇

A dozen scones were more than enough for Angus's dinner that night, so he shoved a small one across the sand to James.

While Angus ate, Fiona came and sat directly in front of him again, watching him closely.

"She's been reading up on you," James said through scone crumbs. "She found a grand lot of books on sea monsters in the library."

"Did she?"

"Aye. And now she thinks you may be able to talk to her." James shook his head sadly. "The poor wee thing's gone daft from too much reading."

"I could talk to her if I wanted to," Angus said.

James said, "Aye, and I'm the queen of Sheba."

"We could all do it, many years ago."

"You were the only animals that could talk to humans, but you took a fancy one day not to do it anymore."

"Yes."

"And why would you do that?"

"We used to live on land, side by side with men. We always treated them as equals, James, even though they were much smaller than ourselves. But then there was some trouble, and we went back into the sea. That was a long time ago, but we still talk about it whenever we swim near shore."

James leaned forward and whispered, "What kind of trouble, laddie?"

"There was a fierce winter . . . so long that it seemed as if there might be no end to it. Every living thing was starving, and dying from the cold. Then one by one the oldest and the youngest members of our family began to disappear. They'd just go grazing and not come back. Ever. And the humans began to stay together, always in groups, and not look at us when we met, and we began to feel . . ." Angus swallowed and looked around him at the gathering darkness.

"Feel what?" James's voice was a whiskery little breath in Angus's ear.

"Followed. Particularly at night, James. Hunted."

James rocked back, blinking.

Angus shivered.

Fiona leaned forward and touched Angus gently on the neck. "The other night I asked you if you could sing, and you did. At least, it sounded like a song to me. Do you remember?"

Angus licked her hand to let her know he did.

She looked into his eyes—a long, deep look. Then she said, slowly, "Sing me that song again."

Angus was dreadfully tired, but nothing was too much trouble if it would please Fiona. He pointed his nose at the sky and began to sing. He put in every verse and every single sound effect. He could feel Fiona's eyes upon him the whole time.

When he was through she jumped up, threw her arms around his neck, and squeezed him tight. "I knew it. You can sing, and you did understand what I said. So it must be true, what they say in the book. You can talk. I'll teach you how. We'll have grand times together, telling each other things."

Angus was greatly astonished. He'd never been hugged before. He liked it. He wondered if Fiona would do it again, if he learned to talk. When she let him go he licked her hand once more. Then he lurched down to the water's edge in a happy daze, and swam home to his island, humming to himself.

◆ ◆ ◆

Fiona was late with breakfast the following morning, and when she did come down the beach, she came slowly. Angus could see she was thinking of something else altogether.

James went to meet her. Angus had learned that James had a great need to be close to his humans—to feel what they felt. James had explained it all to him several times, and once or twice Angus thought he understood it, but then it slipped away from him again.

Fiona put the scones down and sat so she could face

Angus. James lay down close beside her. She said, "The scones aren't very good this morning. I burned them."

Angus had to agree with her. Black scones weren't very good.

Fiona said, "We got a notification in the mail. I was thinking of that instead of the scones."

Angus didn't know how many more of these burned scones he could swallow. He pushed one toward James, who pretended not to see it.

"A long time ago, last fall, Grandfather thought he would order some wee boats to put out in the loch for people to rent. And some picnic tables and benches, too. Because here we are, with the loch and the hills and the fish, and a great need for money. It seemed like a grand idea." She sighed deeply. "But then Grandfather's arthritis got worse, and he was sick all the winter, so now he can't haul a lot of boats about or sit all day in a booth. Even if I helped him every minute, and I would, it'd be too much for him. He might get sick again. I don't want him to get sick." She looked as if she might be going to cry. Angus hoped she wouldn't. He didn't think he could bear it if Fiona cried. All of a sudden he understood what James had been trying to explain to him. He moved closer to her, aching to do something to help.

"Anyway," she said, sniffling, "he wrote the company weeks ago—weeks ago!—telling them he wouldn't be needing the boats and asking could he have his deposit back, but he never heard. And now they say they're sending us the boats and benches, and they're asking for the rest of the money."

She shook her head. "Grandfather phoned the company, and the man was terribly nasty to him. It made me so angry, I wanted to do something horrible to him for talking to my Grandfather like that." Fiona's hands were clenched into two small bony fists and her face was as red as her hair. James, beside her, growled.

Fiona said, "He told Grandfather the boats were on the truck already and couldn't be stopped, that we owed the money and would have to pay. They're coming today."

There was a long silence. Angus didn't know what James and Fiona were thinking, but he was thinking that anyone who worried Fiona's grandfather and made Fiona so angry, should be stopped.

The bit about boats worried him, too. He'd seen a boat once, crossing the ocean. A very large, white thing, moving slowly and sounding as if it were grinding its teeth all the time. The noise from it traveled a long way underwater, and when they heard it and saw the boat on the far horizon, the sea monsters turned in unison like a flock of flying birds and swam in the other direction. Angus knew, from that, that he was to put the ocean between himself and any boat.

Now Fiona was talking about bringing a lot of boats to the loch. He wondered how many of those you could fit into a loch. And if a lot of boats were all packed together on the loch, where would he go? Where could he hide? He looked around in desperation. He was not nearly ready to climb out to the sea. He'd have to retreat to the marsh till he thought of something else.

James said, as if he'd known what Angus was thinking, "If ever they catch sight of you, laddie, they'll be after you with nets or guns."

Angus asked, "How will they come? From which direction?"

"There's only the one road, through the pass. I heard the old man say they'd stop at the house to get their money, then they'll bring the boats down here. You must clear out the moment you hear them."

"I will. Where is the road?"

"Behind the house. Up there, where the sun rises over the hills."

"I'll listen for them, James."

"See you do," James said, darkly, and walked slowly away.

◇ 10 ◇

All day Angus listened. He knew he should go climbing, that every single day counted, but he didn't dare leave Fiona's beach. If those boats came while he was away, he might be trapped at the far end of the loch. Once the loch was filled with boats he wouldn't be able to swim back and forth to climb the mountain anyhow. The boats would change everything.

He thought about Fiona while he waited, and he thought about what he and James might do to stop those men from frightening Fiona and her grandfather. He thought about that a lot.

At suppertime, when the sky overhead was conch pink turning into deep blue, and the loch was a silvery pink mirror, Fiona brought Angus's scones down to the beach. She said, "They must have gotten lost or changed their minds," and she smiled. But James shook his head so only Angus could see him, and looked glum.

Angus had just finished his last crumb when he heard

the truck coming. It was still a long way off, but he could hear it straining up the road to the pass. Now he could see that James had heard it. His ears stood up in sharp points. And finally Angus could see that even Fiona was hearing it. Her voice trailed off and her face went white. She said, "They didn't change their minds."

The three of them waited for the truck in silence. They stood on the beach watching the narrow road that came over Ben Loohie's shoulder. In a few minutes they saw headlights flaring out against the mountain.

James said, "You'd best be away, laddie."

Angus had planned to swim to his island or the marsh the minute the truck came into sight, but now he found he could not leave. Fiona and James might need him. There might be something he could do. He shuffled up the beach and into the trees as quickly as he could, which was not very quickly. James was behind him every step of the way, scolding. "Did I not warn you? Do you want them to see you?"

"They'll not see me. I'll hide in the trees."

James snorted. But he stayed with Angus and found a small bush to sit behind, near Angus's thicket.

The truck came roaring through the trees. It was so big. But not as big as the boat Angus had seen on the ocean, so the boats inside must be very small indeed. Angus sighed with relief.

As the truck came to a stop, Fiona's grandfather walked out of the house and over to the cab. He said,

"Gentlemen, there's been a wee mistake made." Fiona ran to stand beside him.

"Is this the Murray place?" the driver asked. He sounded angry already.

"Aye. I'm Hamish Murray, and this is Fiona Murray, my granddaughter. But we canceled our order a long time ago."

"Don't tell me that. I don't know anything about any cancellation. All I know is they loaded up my truck this morning with boats for Hamish Murray, and they told me to collect . . ." The man flipped through a sheaf of untidy yellow papers. "It's right here, somewhere . . ."

"We just got the notification last night, ourselves," Fiona said, fiercely. "We called right away. And he did so cancel the order—weeks ago."

Her grandfather turned on her. "Hush!"

The driver leaned out the window. "These are your boats, mister, and you owe me some money. Here's the order." He shoved a yellow paper at Hamish. "So sign this and pay me what you owe, and we'll be unloading." He waved the paper in the air impatiently.

Fiona's grandfather did not reach for the order. He stood perfectly still. The driver waited for a moment and then he started to open the cab door as if he were going to make Hamish take it and sign it.

Fiona said, "I've a shepherd's pie in the oven. A lovely big shepherd's pie. I'll just bring you each a plate and you can talk after you eat. Are you not hungry?"

The man in the passenger seat spoke up. "Aye. Let

her bring us a bite of supper, Harry. I'm so hungry I could eat my shoes with sauce. I'm not unloading any boats till I've had something in my stomach."

The driver jammed Hamish's order back into the bunch on the truck dashboard, muttering, "First we have a bum carburetor, then we're lost for an hour, and now we got to eat first."

His partner said, "Aw, Harry . . ."

The driver said, "All right, all right! Bring out the supper. We'll have it here in the cab. But after that we're taking our money, and we're unloading those boats."

Fiona hurried into the house. Hamish followed more slowly, limping. James growled deep in his throat. The fur on his back was up.

Angus said, "If we could make them leave right now, without waiting for their money or unloading the boats, maybe the company would just take the boats back and forget about Hamish and Fiona paying them anymore."

"Aye. And if we had wings, we could live in the trees."

Angus continued, thoughtfully, "I was wondering if people were afraid of very loud, strange noises."

"Indeed, I think so." James looked sharply at Angus. "At least they do not like them. Particularly at night. Night noises make them nervous as cats."

"It's almost night now," Angus said cheerfully. "I have an idea, James."

James said, "Lead on, beastie."

51

It made Angus feel extremely proud and courageous to be talked to like that. He outlined his idea to James.

James's eyebrows went up while he listened. When Angus was through, James said, "Did you think of that yourself?"

Angus nodded modestly.

James said, "Hoosh!" in an admiring way. "Hoosh!"

◇ 11 ◇

Fiona brought out the shepherd's pie, smoking hot in
the cool evening air, and went back into the cottage.
The breeze died down. The loch lay calm under the
stars. It was a very quiet night. Harry and his partner
were busy eating shepherd's pie in the truck.

Angus said, "Now, I think." He began hitching
himself through the underbrush toward a large tree in
back of the truck. He made a good deal of noise moving through those bushes. Small branches broke and
twigs snapped, leaves rustled, and a log rolled downhill.

A flashlight went on inside the cab and a head
popped out one of the truck windows. "Who's out
there?" The flashlight beam swung back and forth in
half-circles through the trees.

Angus stopped moving.

"It's just the old man," the driver said.

"That was no old man."

"He's probably daft, living out here all by himself except for the wee lassie. He probably talks to himself and sees things."

Angus, who talked to himself frequently, ground his teeth. Then he took a deep breath and started in on a recital of all the sounds he had used to scare the fish in the loch. He roared. He screeched. He chattered. He wailed. After a minute or two, he could hear his own echoes coming back at him from all the way across the loch. The whole lochside was full of his noise. It was a proud moment for Angus. Toward the end of Angus's recital, James tilted his head back and howled right along with him.

Angus stopped and waited for the echoes to fade away. Then he peered around his tree. The overhead light in the cab was on and both men had their faces pressed against the rolled-up window on the driver's side. Angus nodded at James. It was going nicely.

He crawled to the middle of the back panel of the truck and nudged it. The truck shivered. One of the men yelled, "Hoi! Who's doing that?"

Angus pushed harder, and a small piece of something fell off the truck.

The cab door on the driver's side opened.

"Don't go out there, Harry!" the other man said.

"Something's hitting the rig in the back. Do you no feel it?"

"Do you want it hitting you as well?"

The cab door slammed shut. The truck headlights went on.

Angus heard another door open. A minute later,

Fiona and Hamish were standing near the truck cab. Fiona was wrapped in a plaid shawl. She and Hamish were holding up lanterns.

Hamish said, "Is anything wrong out here?"

"Go back in the house, old man! And take the wee girl with you. There's something wild out here. . . ." One of the men was whispering through a small opening at the top of the cab window.

"You didn't think you saw a monster, did you?" Fiona asked anxiously. "Because all those stories about sea serpents and water horses and kelpies aren't true. No one believes them anymore. There's nothing at all strange around here, is there, Grandfather? We never see anything."

One of the men rolled the window all the way down. "Look, girlie, there's *something* out here. It's been banging on our truck." He began to open the cab door.

"Now!" Angus whispered to James.

James tilted his head back and began a long, sad series of howls. When he was hitting his highest note, Angus clapped a paw over his mouth, and James stopped short. Then from deep in his chest he brought up a short series of gasping, choking, strangling sounds. Angus had to shake his head in admiration. Anyone who didn't know better would think surely James was dying a horrible death.

Fiona cried, "Oh, my! James?" and whirled around, peering into the bushes. "James?"

The truck engine coughed explosively and started to roar. Angus stepped smartly to one side, shoving James out of harm's way. The truck began to back up. It went over small rocks, big rocks, little bushes, and whole logs. It turned sharply toward the road and moved out. The headlights lit up the track ahead of it and the trees on either side. It went faster and faster, heading for the pass. A few minutes later, it disappeared over Ben Loohie's shoulder, and the loch, the road, and the woods became as quiet and serene as if there had never been a truck there at all.

"James?" Fiona called, frantically. "Are you all right, James?" Hamish whistled sharply several times, turning in a circle.

James trotted over to them.

Fiona said, "Oh, there you are. I was so worried about you!" She bent down to hug him. "I don't think they saw anything else, do you, James?" She held her lantern high. "Is anyone else out there?"

Angus shook his tree lightly, and a few leaves fell off.

"Ah," Fiona said, "everybody's all right, then." She turned back to the cottage. "As long as we're all safe, nothing else matters, does it, Grandfather?" and she disappeared into the house.

Hamish lingered a moment or two, shielding his eyes from his lantern light and looking into the woods. Angus stayed very still, hardly breathing. Finally, the old man shook his head and followed Fiona into the house. James winked at Angus and hurried after him.

At breakfast, next morning, Fiona talked about all

the ways she and her grandfather might cut down on expenses, since they wouldn't be making money from renting boats and they probably wouldn't be getting their down-payment money back, either. There weren't many ways, really. At the end, as she packed up, Fiona grew silent and looked worried.

Angus asked James, "Does she eat fish?"

"Aye. When she catches some. She's no a good fisherman. She's too twitchy . . . always pulling her line in to see has she caught anything. A fish would have to be down there waiting for it, to get to her hook before she yanked it out again."

"If I could get her more fish, would that help?"

"Aye."

"Could you bring her around the shore to that little cove with all the birches, maybe in the middle of the afternoon?"

James nodded.

Angus finished the last crumb of scone. "And see can you get Sarah to come, too."

♦　♦　♦

He saw them starting out. James was in the lead, of course. He would look back over his shoulder and bark, every so often, to keep Fiona coming in the right direction. Sarah was following Fiona. Sarah's tail was high in the air, and her small, precise paws were just barely touching the damp sand.

Angus located a small school of fish, and as James, Fiona, and Sarah came around the point, he herded his school up onto the shore. It was his surprise for Fiona.

Fiona rushed to pick out five or six of the biggest fish. She laid them high on the grass in the shade. Sarah selected one small fish and took it away under a tree, where she enjoyed it right down to the tail. Angus slipped the rest of the fish back into the loch for another day.

◇ 12 ◇

After they all had their scones that evening, and after Fiona had gone away back to her cottage, James sat down facing Angus, and said, "I'm a wee bit worried about you, laddie."

Angus felt icy fear race up his back. "What, James?"

James said, "Every day there are more campers and hikers going by the loch. Did you not notice?"

Angus shook his head.

"And every day you grow a bit bigger. Have you not noticed that?"

Angus shook his head. That was nice to hear, but he had a feeling James didn't think it was good news.

"If any of them should see you and go away home talking about the sea monster that lives in Loch Loohie, they'll be coming here in droves. There might be expeditions to find you, and buses full of sightseers. You wouldn't like it. Fiona says we must never let anyone see you. Never."

Angus shivered. Expeditions? Sightseers?

59

James went on, solemnly. "You must stay out of sight during the day from now on, till it gets cold again. The vacationers go home when it gets cold."

"Won't I see you and Fiona anymore?" Angus asked, feeling shaky and sad.

"Hoosh! Of course you will. We'll just be out for the scones earlier and have our bite of supper later. And we'll keep a sharp eye out for people going by. We'll all watch."

Angus breathed a sigh of relief. Finding a safe spot and hiding in it all day long would be hard. Climbing at night instead of during the day would be harder. But never seeing Fiona and James—that would be terrible. "I'll look for a place to hide in the morning," he promised.

♦ ♦ ♦

The shores of the loch were studded with bushy little thickets and stands of birch and oak trees. Angus knew he could hide in any one of those little thickety places, but he dreaded being out of the water all day. His scales might dry out and shed, which would make him itch all over. And what if he outgrew a smallish hiding place before the cool weather came? What if hikers came along while he was napping and saw a piece of him sticking out? He'd have to find something damper and more substantial than a thicket.

He started swimming along the shore, patiently peering into every shadowy spot. He was snapped at by turtles, scolded by birds, and startled by frogs that jumped into the loch right under his nose. He left a trail of complaints behind him all along the shore.

He was about three-fourths of the way around the loch when he came to a little bog. It wasn't much of a bog, but there were rivulets of fresh water flowing into the loch from it . . . icy cold water that felt so cooling to Angus after his hours of baking in the sun and soaking in the warm surface water of the loch. He turned into one of the rivulets and let the cold water bubble all around him, then he paddled on up the rivulet. It flowed out of a tiny lochan. The lochan was surrounded on three sides by trees, and on the fourth by a cliff. Angus rolled over on his back and floated there for a while, gazing up at the sky. This was very nice—very quiet and private.

A small opening at the base of the cliff caught his eye. He went over to investigate. He poked his head into it and called, "Hello?"

An echo came back to him immediately. He was calling into a cave. It didn't sound as if anyone were home so he swam on in. It was a very large cave with broad stone ledges all around that would be just perfect for a sea monster to rest on.

Angus climbed onto one of the ledges and looked some more. Why, this cave had everything . . . running water, high ceilings, and an almost-hidden entrance.

He sat there a little longer, getting used to being in an enclosed space, then he slipped back into the water and swam out to Loch Loohie. He decided, on the way, to call the lochan Loch Angus.

When he glanced back from Loch Loohie, his new home looked like a bit of bog, a few trees, and a cliff. There were better spots for picnicking or fishing all around the loch. He would be perfectly safe there until the snow fell. Until he could go back to the sea.

◇ 13 ◇

The days were long and warm. Angus would go to his cave after his morning scones and rest on a ledge and watch the watery reflections on his stone ceiling. Sometimes he thought about seeing his family again. Would they even know him at first? Probably not; he had grown so. James said he was more than twice the size he was when he first came to the loch. By the time snow fell he would be very large indeed. And his legs were already thicker and stronger than anybody's—even MacDuff's. He supposed that was because of all the climbing he was doing. He could keep up with James and Fiona now, when they walked along the shore.

More people went by the loch every day. Angus's hearing, sight, and sense of smell were so keen, he knew when strangers were coming long before they actually arrived. A bobby on a bicycle pedaled up and down the road through the pass and shot by the lane to Fiona's place twice a day. He was keeping an eye out for vacationers in difficulty, Fiona said. Small planes came

63

over Ben Loohie and droned back and forth over the loch before they darted away like darning needles. Hikers sweated up and down the hills. Caravans filled to bursting with big families rolled by, and sometimes stopped so the wee ones could cool themselves in the loch. Sheep appeared on the shoulders of Ben Loohie, looking like tiny dots of white fuzz. They would graze a little here and there, and then turn back to other braes where the grass was richer.

The bird found Angus's cave and came to visit him from time to time. Her wing had healed, and she could fly again. One day, as she smoothed down a feather with her beak, she said, "The sun has started south already. The days are getting shorter."

"It's only July," Angus protested. "Fiona said it was July now, and it's still getting warmer."

The bird never argued with him. She just said what she knew to be true. She said, "The sun has started back, Angus. The days are getting shorter."

Angus shivered in spite of the day's warmth.

She noticed. She said, "Will you be ready?"

"I don't know. I'm trying."

She hopped a little closer and brushed his paw with the tip of her wing. "Try harder," she said, and flew off.

◆ ◆ ◆

That evening Angus made up his mind to go beyond the grass and well up into the heather. He set his sights on a certain rock high above the place where he'd stopped the night before.

When he first stepped on the heather, Angus was pleasantly surprised. It was springy, and it tickled. This could be fun. He jumped up and down on it, to see if he could still feel solid ground underneath, and was disappointed to find that he could. But the only way he could walk in the heather was to lift each paw up high and set it down flat on top of the wiry, crisscrossing branches. Clump, clump, clump. It was a very tiring way to walk . . . not so much fun, after all . . . and James said it looked peculiar, too. Very peculiar. Angus thanked him for that bit of information.

James got to the rock before him, of course, and sat down to wait. By the time Angus reached the rock he was exhausted. He hauled himself up onto it with his last bit of strength. "I never thought I'd make it," he said.

"Nor did I," James said, getting to his feet. "Still, there's time to go a wee bit farther."

Angus gave him a look. "This is far enough for tonight."

"I've seen six-week-old puppies go this far, just for the exercise," James said.

Angus's feet were sore. When he thought about it, he realized that there wasn't any part of him that wasn't sore. Furthermore, what James said was absolutely untrue. Six-week-old puppies climbing mountains! He stood up, determined to make James take that back, and he slipped. Before he could right himself, he had tumbled off the rock and was starting to roll down the hill. "Help!" he yelled. "Help me!"

James was at his side in an instant, darting in to get a grip. He bit down hard on Angus's ear and braced himself with all four feet. This slowed Angus down somewhat, but he continued to slide down the hill dragging James with him. They were beginning to pick up speed again when Angus managed to clutch a thorny briar bush as he went by. He wrapped himself around it in an instant and hung on, and they came to a stop.

"Hoi!" James said, and spat out two or three emerald scales.

Angus reached up. His ear was still there. "Ouch!" he said. Then he said, "Thank you, James. If I'd rolled onto you, I'd have crushed you flat."

"Tush!" James said, and started to pick the briars out of his coat.

Angus said, "If you hadn't grabbed me I might have gone all the way down. I might have gone faster and faster till I hit those stones on the shore." He looked down at the beach. It was a long way down. A long way. How far they'd come! Maybe he'd make it over the mountain after all.

Angus's ear was throbbing, and James was limping, when they started home. James said not to worry, he'd be fine in the morning. Angus knew he'd be all right, too. He'd grow more scales.

But James wasn't fine in the morning. Angus found Fiona and his scones waiting for him on the beach, but no James. James hobbled down later, very slowly, as Angus was finishing his breakfast.

For days James was barely able to get around. Angus had to climb by himself, and a lonely business he found it. He brought James the news of the loch every evening—what Tommy and Kipper were up to, and what water birds were arriving and which ones were leaving, and whether or not there were any hare tracks about . . . that kind of thing. Fiona would sit with them and talk to Angus by the hour, repeating over and over all those conversational phrases she thought he might find useful. "Is it time for tea, yet?" "Please pass the sugar." "Please pass the scones." "No more fish, thank you." "Isn't it a lovely day!"

Angus watched Fiona closely, and listened carefully, but he couldn't seem to get his own words out. Sarah would snicker silently, while he tried, and James would hide smiles in his fur. Angus hated to be laughed at. Fiona said he was coming along, but Angus could see that she was getting discouraged, too. Finally, one evening, he left right in the middle of the lesson. He spent the whole next day in the cave asking himself for the sugar and the scones. The harder he tried to talk, the more tied up in knots his tongue and his mind got, till he found himself asking an imaginary someone to pass him a lovely day. His throat was scratchy, and his ears rang from listening to his own echoes in the cave. Angus had had enough. He decided to stop trying to talk. Fiona would be disappointed, of course, but he had tried. And anyway—how much good would all this do him once he was back in the ocean? None.

For four days he skipped his evening lesson. He'd swim by to say hello to James and have a wee snack, but when Fiona sat down to talk about talking, Angus would get up slowly and edge away to the water.

On the fifth day Fiona set out the teapot, and a table-cloth, and several covered plates, which meant they were having a special supper. James limped down, and Sarah swished across the sand for her cream. Angus watched Fiona slather butter and jam on a dozen large, warm scones. His mouth watered as he waited for her to pass the plate.

She gave him a small saucer of cream. Nice, but not filling. James had a large scone.

Fiona gave Angus a little bowl of smoked fish, which was too salty. He ate it, but he didn't really care for it. Sarah loved hers.

James ate another scone, and Fiona had two, with a large cup of tea. Then she put the rest of the scones back in the basket and brought out her book, and settled down to read. Sarah licked Angus's fish dish and started to clean her fur. James hunted for crumbs, then lay down at Fiona's feet.

"She's forgotten me," Angus said to James.

"No, she didn't," James said. "She gave you the fish and the cream."

"You got more cream than I did," Sarah reminded him.

"I'm a lot bigger than you are," Angus retorted.

"You're a lot bigger than anybody is," Sarah said.

"I tell you, she's forgotten me. She's put the scones away."

"Aye," James said.

"Well, can't you do something?"

"You do something," Sarah said.

"And I'd do it soon, if I were you," James said, "while the scones are still warm. Those were the best she's ever made, I think."

Sarah went on working on her fur.

Fiona closed her book with a sigh. "Ah well, no more reading tonight. I must help Grandfather with the butter."

Angus was appalled. She was leaving. All he'd had was a lick of cream and a mouthful of salty old fish. He could smell the scones through the wicker basket. He'd better do something soon or they'd be gone. Very gently, he reached out for the handle of the basket.

Fiona rapped him smartly on the nose with her book. "Out of the basket, Beastie," she said, smiling. "It's so strange. I keep thinking I've forgotten something, but I can't imagine what it is."

Angus was practically dancing up and down now. Of all days for her to forget about him—with butter melting on the best scones she'd ever made, and strawberry jam, too. Fiona turned to leave. It was now or never. Angus closed his eyes to concentrate. "Please pass the scones," he bellowed.

"I knew it!" Fiona shouted. She whirled around and put the basket down and hugged Angus's neck. "And every word clear as a big bell booming! I knew you could do it if only you'd try. I'm so proud of you—and myself, as well."

She handed him the scones as fast as he could eat them. They were absolutely the best he'd ever tasted. And after all those years when no sea monster talked with a human, or even remembered how to, he, Angus, had asked for the scones.

After that it was all talk, talk, talk with Fiona. She told Angus every fairy story she could remember, and gave him a little Scottish history, and passed on wise things her grandfather had said. She admitted to Angus that she'd tried once more to tell her grandfather about him but had only made the old man more angry. "He's afraid, you see, that they might think he's not raising me the way he should. He's awful afraid of that. I'm all he's got, he says." She grabbed Angus and hugged him tight. "But I've got you, haven't I?"

Angus told her about the sea, and his trips through the underwater passageway and down the river. Fiona got so worried at the point when he had thought he was trapped underwater she turned quite pale, and he had to remind her instantly that it had come out all right— because after all, here he was. He also told her about his plan to climb the mountain. She was terribly impressed, and against it completely, because, she said, he was sure to fall and kill himself.

Angus found he could pronounce almost anything except *L*s. He was exceptionally good with *S*s, and he could handle almost all the other letters, but when he put his tongue up to the roof of his mouth to make an *L*, he had too much tongue left over, and his *L*s sounded more like *R*s, which meant that he said things like "*Erroch Errhoohie*" instead of "Loch Loohie." Sarah thought this was very funny and snickered a good bit. When he was particularly tired and discouraged about his *L*s, Angus thought how nice it would feel to step on a small piece of Sarah while she was laughing at him— the tip of her tail, perhaps, or one of her toes.

He continued to climb. He hated to worry Fiona, but over the mountain was the only way home, so over the mountain he must go. When James had recovered from his strain, he climbed with Angus again. Angus was so glad of his company that no matter what James said about how slowly Angus was moving or how often he stopped to rest, Angus just smiled . . . which irritated James intensely.

◇ 14 ◇

The days were still long. After the sun winked out in the west, there was a soft, slow deepening of the darkness. There would be a few hours of real night, and then the sky in the east would brighten and a new day would start. Angus had to wait until it was so dark he could hardly be seen against the grass or the heather. Then he and James would hurry, hurry, hurry up the mountain. They'd pile some stones in a wee cairn when they'd gone as high as Angus could climb that night, and then they'd hurry, hurry, hurry down to the shore.

When curtains of rain swept down the loch, Angus could go visiting or climbing all day long. He blended into the wet green very nicely, and clouds would come down with the rain and wrap long white veils around the mountains.

He had just gotten back to his cave, one rainy day, when Kipper and Tommy came by. Tommy asked him to go sliding with them.

Angus said no. He was too tired to go anywhere. Not today.

"But we're building a lovely new slide," Tommy said, "and we thought that if you would . . ."

Kipper cuffed him on the back as if he were choking. Tommy certainly did choke then, and it took him some time to get his breath back.

"It won't take long," Kipper said. "We'd like you to be the first one to try our slide, because you are our favorite other animal."

Angus said, "I'll come and see it tomorrow. It's very nice of you to ask." Privately he was wondering what a slide was and how you tried it out.

Tommy said, "But if you don't go down first, it . . ."

Kipper slapped him on the back again, harder, and said, "You must stop eating nettles if they make you choke like that."

"If I don't go down first what . . . ?" Angus demanded.

Kipper made a face. "The thing is, Angus, we need someone really big and heavy to clear something away and smooth the slide down, and we knew you'd be tired, so . . ."

"Oh."

"But you'd enjoy it as well. It isn't as if you wouldn't enjoy it."

Angus started to say he absolutely would not enjoy it if it meant walking anywhere, but Tommy stood up on his hind legs and peered anxiously into Angus's face and said, "Please come, Angus."

Angus groaned, and rolled off the ledge into the water. "Once," he said. "I'll do it once. That's all."

The otters led the way, chattering with excitement.

The slide was on a bank that sloped steeply into the loch. A dead tree had fallen on the bank years ago, killing the grass and weeds that lay underneath it. The otters had managed to roll the trunk a few inches to one side, exposing the mud underneath—a clear track from the top of the bank into the water. So that's what a slide was. Angus understood, now.

He leaned against the log and it rolled several feet more. Tommy was thrilled. "Look at that! He just touched it, almost, and it went rolling away."

Kipper said, "If you really don't want to go down, Angus . . ."

Angus said, "I said I'd go down once. Once."

He climbed to the top of the bank. Each of his scales was attached at the front and loose toward the rear, so he would have to slide headfirst. His hump would get in the way if he went down on his back, so he'd have to lie on his stomach. Angus was positioning himself very carefully at the top of the slide, arranging his scales just so, when without any warning he found himself on his way down the bank, picking up speed as he went. Tommy and Kipper shouted encouragement as he flashed past. He hit the water hard. Quite a lot of it went up his nose, and a great fountain rose and fell around him. As soon as his head cleared, Angus started up the bank again.

"Oooh, he's going down again!" Tommy exclaimed, dancing around Kipper. "And just look how smooth it is already."

This time Angus went even faster, and he made sure he was blowing air out of his nose when he hit the water. It was a grand ride—short, but exciting. He started up the bank for a third go-round.

"Here!" Kipper said, "You wait your turn," and he flung himself onto the slide and swooshed down into the water.

"Everybody's had a slide but me," Tommy said. "It's my turn now. Get out of the way, Kipper."

"I am out of the way."

"You aren't. You're too close in."

The discussion about whether or not Kipper should move continued. Angus climbed quietly into position behind Tommy, at the head of the slide.

Kipper said, "I say I'm not too close, and I say I'm staying right here."

Tommy said, "I can't have a proper turn with you there. I'm likely to run into you."

Angus pushed off, snatching Tommy and holding him close to his chest as they plummeted down the slide together. Tommy screeched like a banshee all the way down. They hit the water inches away from Kipper, who definitely was too close for his own good.

It took Tommy and Kipper some time to stop coughing. The ringing in Angus's right ear, which had been only inches away from Tommy's mouth, took an hour or so to fade away. But Angus couldn't remember when he'd had so much fun. Over and over he went down the otter slide.

He would have to tell everybody about this when he got back to the ocean. And Tommy and Kipper—he would like to tell everyone about them, too.

75

One evening, as they were having their scones, Fiona said, "I've never seen where you spend the days, Angus."

"It's just a cave."

"I know, but I've never seen it. May I come?"

Angus didn't know what to say. His cave suited him, but he knew that it would look like a hole in a cliff to anyone else. Not like Fiona's cottage, at all. He'd been in her house one day when her grandfather was away looking after his cows. It was very cozy. There were several comfortable-looking old chairs which sagged nicely in the middle to fit the people who sat in them, and there was a shiny kettle on a black stove, and there were pots with pink flowers in them at the windows. He said, "There's nothing to see. It's just a cave."

But Fiona was determined. "I'll bring tea, and a surprise. We'll have a tea party." She started to collect her things. "So that's settled, then. But how will we find our way in?"

Angus said, "I'll take you. Row down the loch to the wee bog, and I'll meet you there."

"Lovely!" Fiona said. "We'll come just before the sun sets." She had bought a very old, flat-bottomed boat for herself and her grandfather with money she'd saved from selling extra fish whenever Angus held a cove party. She had rechristened it *The Mary, Queen of Scots*, and painted it bright red. She was very proud of it.

There wasn't much Angus could do to get the cave ready for company. He did brush the fish scales off the ledges, and he widened one of the rivulets for Fiona's boat. He hoped that it would stay sunny late so she could see the reflections on his ceiling.

He saw them starting out and went to meet them at the bog. When he took the mooring rope in his mouth, Fiona pulled in her oars and leaned back. "I just love parties," she said, and sighed with contentment.

A few minutes later she was climbing out of her boat onto a ledge in the cave. From the bottom of the boat, she brought a brown teapot under a bright red tea cozy, a blue-and-white checkered tablecloth, cups, plates, sugar and cream, oatcakes, and a very large something wrapped in clean white dish towels.

"Now," she said, "since this is to be a tea party, I made something special." She whipped off the dish towels. There lay a giant scone dripping with melted butter and jam, studded all over with raisins. Angus had never seen the like.

James came to attention, and Sarah walked all around it once, sniffing.

"It weighs ten pounds if it weighs an ounce," Fiona said.

There was a sudden ripple of water in the cave, and a small splash. James growled softly. Tommy's head popped up beside the ledge. Fiona gave a small scream.

"It's all right," Angus said. "He's an otter . . . a friend." He turned to Tommy. "Where's Kipper?"

"He wanted to come in. He smelled that, too." Tommy nodded at the scone. "But he said it wouldn't be suitable." Tommy eyed Sarah and James warily. "It is suitable, isn't it, Angus?"

"Yes. Tell him to come in and have a bit of scone." Tommy disappeared.

"I've never seen an otter that close before," Fiona whispered. "Do they bite?"

Angus sighed. "Only each other," he said.

A moment later, two glistening brown heads appeared beside the ledge.

"I didn't want to come," Kipper told Angus, "but he would have it."

"Would you like a piece of scone?" Angus said. He pushed a plate with several large slices of scone on it close to the otters. "Fiona made it specially . . ." The plate was bare and two small swirls of disturbed water showed where the otters had been.

"Tea?" Fiona asked Angus.

"You got more raisins than I did!" The complaint could be heard quite clearly inside the cave, although by now the otters were certainly outside in the lochan. "You picked the piece with the most raisins."

"How many raisins did you get?" It sounded like Kipper talking, trying to be reasonable.

"This many."

"Well, that's how many I've got."

"But you already ate some. I saw you."

78

"Will you be quiet!" Kipper said. "Here's another raisin."

Tommy said, "You gave me a shriveled one."

"They're all shriveled."

"That one's not," Tommy said.

"Here! You let go of my scone!"

"I'll let go of your scone." Tommy sounded really angry. "I'll let go of it. See if I don't!" Then Angus heard a sound very much like a large piece of scone hitting the water. Immediately the confused clamor of an otter fight broke out—chattering, squealing, and sloshing.

"Yes," Angus said, calmly, "I'll have some tea."

"And an oatcake?" Fiona asked, although her eyes were on the entrance to the cave.

Angus heard thrashing and splashing outside as if someone's head were being held under water by another someone.

"Yes. I'd like an oatcake," he said. "This scone is the best I ever ate."

James, his whiskers liberally sprinkled with pale crumbs, nodded agreement.

"Do you know why I really wanted to have a party this evening?" Fiona asked. "It's three months today that James found you beside the loch. Three months." She reached over and hugged Angus. "So, this is your anniversary tea party, Angus. Surprise!"

He *was* surprised. Three months. That sounded like a long time. Sometimes it seemed to Angus as if James had found him beside the loch just the other day. He could remember that morning so clearly. At other times he felt as if he'd always lived in the loch, and the sea was just a dream he'd had.

He leaned forward and licked Fiona's cheek. It tasted salty, like the sea. "Thank you, Fiona," he said, "and thank you, James. And Sarah. Thank you for . . ." And then, because everyone was embarrassed by what he or she was feeling, they all got busy loading the boat for the return trip, and Angus's anniversary tea party was over.

◇ 15 ◇

The bird was waiting for him one morning when he came out of his cave. Angus hauled himself out of the water onto the grass. "Good morning, bird."

"Good morning."

"How are you?"

"Very well. I'm almost ready. I've been practicing, too."

"Ready for what?" Angus asked, although he thought he knew.

"For going south."

A twinge of unhappiness rippled through Angus's insides. "No," he said. "It's too early to go south."

"Soon."

"How soon?" he demanded.

"A few weeks."

Angus looked around him. Suddenly he saw that while he'd been sleeping days and climbing nights, summer, with all its gentle greens, had gone. The bracken on the hills was burning with a tawny gold color. The heather was staining the mountainside a deep rosy purple. The grass was rusty red. He turned away from the mountains. "There's plenty of time yet," he said.

"I can feel the coldness coming in the sky, Angus."

"It's warm enough down here," he grumbled.

She didn't answer.

"I'm up to the rocks, now," he said.

"I know."

"How do you know?"

She said, "I watch you. I see you leaving as it gets dusky, and coming back as the sun rises over the mountain. I hear you talking to James and Fiona."

Angus said, "I never see you."

"You're not watching for me." She sang a little trill that sounded like Fiona's laughter. "And you're a great deal easier to see than I am."

"Well anyhow, I'm up to the rocks," he said, again.

"And the rockslides," she said softly. "That's what I wanted to talk to you about."

Angus waited, feeling cold. The rockslides frightened him. If a big slide started above him, it could roar down on him before he could get away, and carry him with it clear to the foot of the mountain, burying him forever. But sometimes picking his way across the apron of a slide seemed easier and maybe even safer than climbing around a jumble of giant boulders.

"Don't climb the rocks in the dark," the bird said.

"I'll be seen in the day. I'm so big now. Do you want me in a cage somewhere, or shot at?"

"The rocks are too dangerous at night."

Angus shook his head. "Not as dangerous as some other things, bird."

With a whisper of flight she was gone, brushing his shoulder with her wing.

Angus stared into the water for a long time. The bird was right. She was always right. Already, although she couldn't know this because it happened at night, he'd set off one small slide. It did not turn into a big one and take him with it—but he'd had a close call. How could he risk climbing by day? He was bright blue and green and white—and big as a cottage, as well. Someone would be sure to see him standing against the gray mountain rock. No. It was better to take his chances with the rockslides at night than to risk being seen in the day.

◆ ◆ ◆

Several weeks later, the policeman came by to say he'd see Fiona and her grandfather in the spring. Most of the vacationers had gone back to work, and he was being reassigned to school crossings. Fiona watched him go till he was out of sight.

"It's a wee bit lonely here in the winter," she said to Angus. "Grandfather teaches me my lessons, and there are James and Sarah . . ." She sighed. Then she said, "Ah, well . . . Grandfather wants me to air the blankets while the sun's out, so I must be getting back to the house."

Angus shuffled down to the loch. The policeman was

gone, and most of the vacationers . . . and Fiona was airing blankets. In the mornings, now, the air was chilly. He glanced up at the mountain and shivered. Time was running out. But he and James would be able to climb in the daytime again. That was something to be glad about.

◇ 16 ◇

They were climbing over some tremendous rocks, the following day, when James sat down suddenly with a tiny whimper. Angus had never heard James whimper before. He turned back, concerned. "What is it, James?"

"I can go no farther, laddie."

"Did you slip? Are you hurt?"

"No. I just can't keep up with you any longer."

"Oh." Angus sat down beside James. "I'll wait. There's plenty of time."

James said, "You'll have to go on without me, from here. I'm no up to it."

Angus didn't know what to say. He'd never dreamed that he, Angus, would be able to climb higher than James some day. At last he said, "It's your legs, James. You've got such short legs that while I'm taking just the one step, you're taking ten. If we rest for a few more minutes, you'll—"

"That'll do no good—no good at all," James said, irritably.

"Are you angry with me?" Angus asked.

"No, laddie. Don't be thinking that." There was a long silence. Then James said, "I'll wait here. You must go the rest of the way yourself. See that you go slow. Take care with each step."

Angus set off across the next jumble of rocks. It wasn't the same without James. It was never the same.

♦ ♦ ♦

The bird was waiting for him that afternoon when he came back from tea and scones. It was getting dark early now, and Angus was surprised to see her at his cave when she should have been finding her perch for the night.

She said, "I've something to tell you, Angus."

All of a sudden he had that awful feeling in his stomach. "What's wrong?"

"Nothing's wrong. Everything is as it should be. I flew north today, and there was snow on the mountaintops."

"Snow?" He'd known right away it must be something he didn't want to hear. "How far away?"

"Not far, Angus."

"Oh."

There was a long silence. Then she said, "And the whales are coming. I saw them, today, too."

Angus knew what that meant. The whales were on their way to warmer waters. The sea monsters would be practicing formation swimming already, preparing to fall into line behind the whales in the great procession of migration. Big, little, big, little, nose to tail, nose to tail.

When he looked up, the bird was gone. Just once, he thought, he'd like her to stay for a while, and talk a little about this and that, and say, "Good-bye," three or four times before she actually went. He never had a chance to just chat with her . . . to get to know something about her. She appeared like a falling leaf, and disappeared like a shadow.

Snow. Not far away. She'd be leaving for good, soon.

The longer he thought about that, the more depressed he felt. He was afraid he'd start howling if he kept it up much longer, so he plunged into the loch. A long, hard swim would leave him too tired to think. He'd go to sleep and it would be time for breakfast when he woke up. That would cheer him.

◆ ◆ ◆

It was only a few days later that the bird woke him by tapping briskly on his head with her beak.

"Hoi!" Angus cried, rubbing his head. "That hurts!"

"I'm sorry. You were very sound asleep."

"I was tired, bird. I climbed a long way yesterday."

"That's good." She stood there, looking up at him soberly, so tiny that he could have blown her away with one breath, and then she said, "I'm going, now."

"Going where?" he asked, although he knew, and it made his stomach hurt.

"South."

"Already?"

"Not 'already,' Angus. It's time. It's time for us to go—you and me. I can feel a change coming."

"What kind of change?"

"Snow."

"Hoosh!" Angus said. "Are you sure?"

"Yes."

"Hoosh!" Angus said again. "But you aren't going today."

"Yes, I am."

"And am I to go today, too?" Suddenly Angus felt frightened. Today? He wasn't ready today.

"Tomorrow." The bird stirred, rearranged her feathers, and hopped to the mouth of the cave. "Thank you, Angus."

"For what?"

"For saving my life."

"Please don't go, bird," he begged.

"I must."

"I'll miss you," Angus said, sadly.

"Will you leave tomorrow? Do you promise?"

"Yes. I think I can do it. When I stopped yesterday I could see the top clearly."

"Then you'll be all right."

"How about the other side of the mountain? Is it very steep?"

"Very. But you've only to go down that side once. Don't look down if you feel dizzy. Look just at the place where you are."

Angus nodded. "I wish you were going to go with me, to help."

The bird thought that over. "I can help."

Angus's heart bounced. "How?"

"I can give you a thing to do that will keep you from taking a wrong step."

Angus believed her. There had always been something special and wise about the bird.

She said, "When you are standing on the highest rock, stop, turn around, and look behind you. Count the number of faces turned toward you. Hold that number in your heart."

"I just count and remember that number?" Angus asked. "Don't you have a thing for me to carry, bird, or maybe some special words to say?"

"No. Just that. It will be enough."

Angus said, "Fiona has a four-leaf clover, and James has a lucky bone, and Sarah has a feather—she left it here, somewhere, the other day. . . ." and he started to poke around in the corners of the ledge for the feather.

When he turned back the bird was gone. Maybe he shouldn't have mentioned Sarah's having a lucky feather. Maybe, if you were talking to a bird, that wasn't suitable. He lashed his tail from side to side in regret and frustration. He'd never even gotten to say good-bye properly.

"Good-bye, bird," he shouted out the mouth of the cave, just in case she could still hear him. "Good-bye!"

And he thought, although he was never, ever sure, that he heard a clear, sweet trill rippling down through the morning sky.

◇ 17 ◇

Angus spent the rest of the day visiting, telling every-one he would be going over the mountain the next day, and saying good-bye. The otters were full of admiration for anyone who had climbed that high. Tommy won-dered out loud what it would be like to stand way up there, and he asked Kipper if he would like to try it. Kipper said, "No, and neither would you," and began to talk about something else with Angus. Tommy went away a few paces, muttering, then he turned and made faces at Kipper behind his back. When Angus started to leave, Tommy ran back and grabbed him around the leg. "Don't go, Angus."

"I have to go. I have to say good-bye to Fiona, and James, and Sarah."

Tommy let go. When Angus looked back, the otters were sitting side by side, watching him swim away.

♦ ♦ ♦

Fiona and James insisted that they would go as far as they could up the mountain with Angus, in the morn-

90

ing. Fiona baked an extra recipe of scones, to strengthen him, and James went over all the things they'd learned about safe climbing. When tea was served, Sarah pushed her cream toward Angus. "I shouldn't have cream, today," she said. "I'm getting fat. A cat should never be fat."

Angus looked at her. There wasn't an ounce of fat anywhere on Sarah. But he accepted her cream graciously, without an argument.

As he swam across the loch toward his cave he realized that the sky had become overcast. Not a single star blinked through. The wind had swung around to the north. Angus reminded himself that he'd seen many a cloudy night come and go without snow falling.

He dreamed a lot that night. Once or twice he woke suddenly, startled by something he couldn't remember in his dream. By the time the eastern sky turned gray, Angus was glad to be getting up.

There was a sudden commotion outside—a wild chattering and splashing. Tommy came streaking through the water into the cave and leaped onto Angus's ledge squalling, "Angus! Are you still here, Angus? Angus!"

Angus had to hold him down and give him a wee shake to calm him. "What's wrong? Tell me slowly. Tell me!"

"Kipper's in a poacher's trap. His leg's all bloody, and I can't get him loose. He doesn't even speak to me anymore. What can we do? What can we do? Kipper's in a trap!"

"Show me."

Tommy slipped out of Angus's grasp and was off, slicing through the water like a brown snake. Angus could hardly keep him in sight.

When Tommy pulled out onto a bank and Angus caught up with him and saw Kipper, he knew this was bad. This was enough to make anyone squall. Kipper's leg was caught between the jaws of a trap. He had torn up the ground around the trap trying to free himself. Now he lay limp beside it, his eyes closed, his fur streaked with dirt and blood.

"Kipper," Tommy said, snuffling, "Angus is here."

Kipper opened his eyes and raised his head a little. Angus could tell he knew they were there. Then Kipper let his head drop with a whimper.

Angus forced himself to look at the trap, not at Kipper. He studied it carefully. It seemed to him that if he shoved his own big paw between the jaws of the trap and forced them apart, Kipper could be lifted away.

"You get down there by his head," he said to Tommy. "When I say, 'Pull,' you pull, but gently. If I say, 'Stop,' you stop right away."

"It won't hurt him, will it, when I pull?"

"Not if you wait till I say to."

"And it won't get me instead, will it, Angus?"

"No."

"Or you? It can't catch you, can it?"

Angus shivered. "No. I don't think so. Get ready."

Angus placed the hard edge of his paw between the two pieces of cold steel and began to press . . . very slowly . . . very carefully. He watched Kipper for any sign that he was feeling more pain. At first nothing happened. Angus began to wonder if he was doing the right thing. Then, as he pressed harder, the metal jaws began to separate. Angus put more weight on the trap. It creaked loudly, and opened wide.

"Now!" Angus said. "Lift his leg and pull him away. Pull."

Tommy worked as gently and skilfully as Fiona would have done. Angus could hear him making little grunts of effort and concentration. In a minute, Kipper was free, lying on his side on the ground, far away from the trap.

Angus took a deep breath and pulled his own paw out of the trap. The trap snapped shut with a nasty clang. Angus slapped the trap sideways, and it leaped out of the ground and skittered away over the dry grass. He walked over to it, picked it up between his teeth, and hurled it far out into the loch.

Tommy was bent over Kipper. "Will he be all right, Angus?"

Angus didn't know. He'd never seen anyone hurt like this before. They needed Fiona, and her grandfather's salves. They needed her right away. He knew he couldn't take Kipper to Fiona by swimming with him across the loch. And there wasn't time to carry him all the way around the loch, either. Kipper would have to be handled gently, carefully . . . not dragged about from pillar to post.

Angus said, "Tommy, you lie down beside him, as close as you can get. Keep the wind off him. I'll get help."

Tommy lay down and curled himself around Kipper

like an outer wrapping. "You'll be back again soon, won't you, Angus?" he asked. "You're coming back, aren't you?"

"I'm bringing Fiona. She'll know what to do." He could see that Tommy was trembling. He reached over and gave the top of Tommy's head a comforting lick. Then he surged into the water and started swimming as he'd never swum before in his life.

Fiona had put down the mixing bowl she was holding before Angus finished telling her about Kipper. She wrapped her red plaid shawl about her and packed a square wicker basket with tins of salve and bottles of a dark liquid and pieces of clean white cloth. Her hands moved like flickering shadows. A minute later, she was shoving *The Mary, Queen of Scots* into the water and tossing the mooring rope to Angus, who took it between his teeth and lunged into the loch.

Tommy got up when he saw Fiona coming. He retreated to a bush a few feet away while she examined Kipper, but his eyes never left her.

When Fiona had finished cleaning and wrapping Kipper's wounds, she bundled him up in her shawl and laid him gently in the bottom of the boat. "He'll need more nursing, Angus," she said, "and lots of nourishment, and keeping warm for a bit. You must take us home as fast as you can."

Angus towed the boat home while Tommy swam alongside.

An hour or so later, Fiona came out of her cottage

94

and walked down to where Angus was waiting. "I've put him in a pen out back, where Grandfather used to keep the early lambs. It's very sheltered."

"Will he be all right, do you think?"

"I think so. He's come round nicely." Her hands dropped to her sides. "I don't know, Angus. I've done everything I can think of, but that trap did an awful injury to his wee leg." She shook her fist in the air. "Ooh! It was the poachers did this! I'd like to put them in a trap." Her fists came down. She said, "Angus, have you looked at the sky?"

"There's not enough time left for me to go today."

"Aye," she said. "You've got to be able to see where you're going, especially going down to the sea on the other side. You couldn't do that in the dark."

"I'll go tomorrow morning."

Fiona shook her head. "It'll be snow by tomorrow," she whispered, and she glanced up as she spoke, as if she were afraid the clouds might hear her.

"What else could I do?" Angus asked. "I couldn't leave them."

When Angus went behind Fiona's cottage to see Kipper he found Tommy already in the pen with him. Tommy was chattering with fright, but he had to be with Kipper. Angus leaned over the side of the pen. "Tommy, are there more traps still out there?"

"Oh, yes. We knew about most of them, but this was a new one. We don't have your sense of smell, Angus. No one does."

Angus remembered how sharp and unpleasant the

odor of the trap had been to him. He'd know that smell again. Oh, yes. "Tell me where to look," he said.

The first trap was the hardest to find. After that he knew what to look for, and his nose served him well. Whenever he found a trap, he yanked it free and set it on a rock where he could grind it beneath his paw till it was twisted out of shape. Then he picked it up with his teeth and sent it whistling through the air to drop into the loch. Ten traps . . . eleven . . . twelve. He came around a small clump of bushes, nose to the ground, and reared up in surprise. "James!"

James said, "I was keeping an eye on those two in the lambs' pen, and I heard a noise. I said to myself, 'Is it the rock slides you're hearing? . . . because there's nothing around the loch sounds like that.' So I came out to have a look, and saw you poking about here and there, finding something, and roaring away over it."

"I was roaring?"

"Aye. You'd be pounding something into the ground and roaring the while. It was a grand thing to watch. Was it the traps you were after?"

"Yes. I think I've gotten the lot."

James nodded approval. "The poachers will think the water bailiff is on to them. There's no profit in putting out traps that disappear into the loch, and never a bit of fur coming back. They'll move on." He studied the sky for a minute. Then he said, "Any other day they could have gotten themselves trapped, but it must be today. Do you not smell the snow?"

"They couldn't help it. Kipper didn't want to get trapped."

"You agreed not to go once it was snowing."

"I have to go tomorrow. It'll not get any better, James. Only worse. More snow. More ice."

For a minute or two, James didn't answer. Then he said, "Ah well, maybe that idiot Tommy will fall on his head. That'll stop you."

◇ 18 ◇

Angus spent another long night dreaming and waking suddenly in terror. Finally he got up and went to the mouth of his cave to wait for the dawn. The sky was just beginning to lighten, but the ground was already white. Snow was swirling around the entrance to his cave, doing a spiraling dance over the black water. Angus groaned. The snow hadn't waited for him.

He looked around the cave for the last time. It had been his home and he would miss it. Then he slipped into the water and headed for Fiona's beach.

Smoke was rising over the trees. He remembered his first breakfast with Fiona—how he had been practically starving, and she had saved him with her scones.

They ate silently. Angus longed to be saying all those things that were jumbling around in his mind, but he felt too awkward. It was hard to say some things right out loud.

The snow stopped as they finished breakfast. Fiona wrapped herself in layers and layers of shawls and put on a pair of Wellingtons, and the three of them set off. Sarah stayed home. The only things Sarah climbed were trees. Angus understood.

The snow was fluffy and dry—not slippery as Angus had feared. James said that was because it was so very cold. Fiona's nose and cheeks got red, and her blue eyes watered till she was obliged to cover most of her face with a shawl and keep her head down.

They came up over the big meadow three abreast. Angus looked back and saw a white field with three lines of brown tracks trailing away behind them. Every so often, they would pass a wee cairn of stones Angus and James had left as a marker, and each one would remind Angus of the day they had put it there.

Fiona had to stop and rest more often now. Angus knew she could not go on much farther. The wind and the cold were cruel.

When they reached the top of the moor, he said, "Fiona, will you not wait here in the shelter of this rock, and let James and me go on alone?"

Fiona just looked at him. Angus kissed her cheek quickly and rushed on into the heather.

As he and James trudged on, the snow would flurry down, then die away, and then come back again. Angus could feel the wind swinging into the west. Now, instead of getting colder, higher up, the air began to feel warmer. They were going over the lowest rocks when Angus slipped for the first time. He caught himself, and then he sat down to rest and steady himself.

"It's getting warmer," James said.

"Aye."

"We'll have to go slower."

They went on, not talking now because they needed all their breath for climbing. James slipped several times so Angus insisted that James go ahead. That way Angus could catch him if he took a bad fall. There was no chance that James could stop, or even slow down, someone Angus's size if he should fall.

Finally, about halfway over the rocks, James stopped. He was all done in.

Angus said, "You've gone as far as ever you went before."

"I had it in my mind to go all the way to the top."

"I wouldn't have let you. How could I leave you up there with no one to see you safely down?"

"Go slow," James implored him. "Be careful. If you cannot make it, it'll be no disgrace."

"I'll be careful, James. But I cannot go too slow."

James crept into the lee of a ledge and settled down. Angus went on alone.

Now he was so high it was frightening to look down. He had to pick his way cautiously. The snow at this height was a lot deeper, and under the western wind it was becoming ever more slippery. Sometimes, a wild, warm gust of wind hit him as he crossed an exposed piece of rock and he had to crouch down and wait for the wind to blow itself out. The day was more than half gone . . . he could tell by the brightness that should have been the sun . . . but he dared not go any faster.

He was nearly at the top now. Up here, a hard, clear

shine on the rocks reflected the light. Here was ice, more dangerous than any snow. He avoided the shiny areas when he could, but sometimes he had to cross them.

He was having trouble breathing. The air was too thin for a creature who lived at or below sea level. He felt constantly out of breath, and even stopping to rest did not help anymore. His paws were numb from the cold. He ached from catching himself each time he started to fall. This last bit, where he had never been before—this was the hardest part of all.

Suddenly, without warning because he had been concentrating so hard on the rock just in front of each paw, Angus reached a spot where there was no more rock above him. Just sky.

He was at the top.

◇ 19 ◇

Slowly Angus straightened up. The ocean lay below him, spreading all the way out to the horizon. It went on and on and on. You could swim forever out there and never have to stop—never even have to turn around. The size of it—the wildness of it—made Angus tremble. The familiar smell of it filled his nose. He breathed in deeply.

There were no signs of whales or sea monsters, but he knew they were there somewhere, just under the surface.

Then he remembered the bird's instructions. He was to turn around and count all the faces turned toward him. Would there be any? He was afraid to look. What would he do if there weren't any faces?

Cautiously, because he felt quite dizzy, he turned.

He could see James—a small, black lump sheltered under the ledge, peering up at him. One.

Down on the moor he saw Fiona. She was waving one of her shawls at him. She should be staying in the lee of that boulder, he thought, and she shouldn't have taken off that shawl. Fiona, with her salves and her books and her ten-pound raisin scone. Two.

To his surprise, on the shore in front of Fiona's cottage he saw a small, rusty spot—an orange cat, a cat who loved warmth and dryness, sitting in the snow on a cold, windy beach. Sarah. He'd never have thought Sarah would be watching him. Three.

He looked for Fiona's cottage among the trees. Behind the cottage in a pen two little brown coils were pointed toward him. The otters. If he'd left one day earlier . . . if he hadn't been there . . . Kipper would still be lying beside the loch, covered with snow. And Tommy would still be waiting for him to wake up. Angus shivered. Tommy and Kipper. Five.

The number he must remember was five. He turned back toward the ocean. Five.

For a long moment he stood there, staring at the ocean as if he had never seen it before. It was just as he remembered it . . . it was as it had always been . . . as it would always be, whether there were sea monsters in it or not.

For a few minutes he clung to a pillar of rock beside him. He needed something solid to cling to. He'd worked for this moment month after month, never doubting he should risk everything for it, never giving up. Now, after all the struggling, after nights of sad dreams and hours of daydreaming, he was not sure any longer.

He turned back toward the loch. That wasn't true.

He was sure. He thought back to those first days in the loch when he had called until his voice gave out. Never once had he heard a call coming back to him from the ocean. Now five silent calls were reaching up to him from the lochside.

Angus took one more long, long look at the ocean. Then he started back down toward the loch.